ANIMALS YOU WILL NEVER FORGET

Written by Alice Leonhardt

STECK-VAUGHN
ELEMENTARY · SECONDARY · ADULT · LIBRARY

A Harcourt Company

www.steck-vaughn.com

Contents

Introduction

Animals have been important to humans since the beginning of time. Long ago people depended on animals for food and clothing. It wasn't long before one animal, the wolf, became a friend to people. Dogs of today come from some early wolves. Cats have also been partners with humans for thousands of years. Cats were once so important in Egypt that Egyptians worshipped them.

As thousands of years passed, people learned a lot about dogs and cats. They also learned about many other animals. Today we are still learning about the creatures living on our planet. They teach us about our world and ourselves. Some of these animals are so special that we will never forget them.

Cuddles
A Little Horse with a Big Job

Cuddles is only 2 feet (61 centimeters) tall and fuzzy. She wears tiny sneakers on her 4 feet. Her job is to guide Dan Shaw, her **visually impaired** owner, around malls, down busy sidewalks, and up steps. Amazing? Definitely. But what's even more amazing is that Cuddles is a horse!

She is a **miniature** horse, to be exact. Cuddles is the first guide horse trained by the Guide Horse Foundation and placed with an owner. Actually, she's the first guide horse *ever*. Guide dogs have been trained to assist the visually impaired for more than 70 years.

Janet and Don Burleson, who started the Guide Horse Foundation, were the first ever to consider using miniature horses.

Why use miniature horses instead of dogs? There are many reasons, the Burlesons explain. One reason is that horses can live more than 20 years longer than dogs. That was one of the main reasons Dan Shaw chose Cuddles.

Miniature horses are also easy to take care of. They do need grooming and bathing, just as dogs do. However, they shed only two times a year. Miniature horses don't get fleas either. Another reason is that many people who are **allergic** to dogs are not allergic to horses.

One more reason is that horses eat grass, hay, and oats, so they cost less to feed than a dog. They also make great miniature lawnmowers! Guide horses are a good choice for people who don't want an animal living in the house. Dan Shaw has built a barn and corral for Cuddles, even though she has a room of her own in the Shaws' house. Cuddles is also housebroken!

Another reason why miniature horses make good guide animals is that they have a calm personality.

During Cuddles' eight-month training, she was introduced to many loud and scary sounds. Now, if Cuddles does get scared, she won't run away. Cuddles is so calm that on a recent round-trip airplane flight, she stretched out on the floor and took a nap.

Horses are natural guide animals. Cuddles naturally watches out for danger and finds the safest route. That's because wild horses need to be alert and smart to survive. Guide horses are trained to avoid moving **obstacles** such as cars and bikes. They are also taught to watch out for high or low things in their path.

Cuddles is calm even on an airplane.

On their first trip together, Cuddles and Shaw went into a crowded store in Raleigh, North Carolina. "We never bumped into anything the whole time," Shaw says. "It was like having eyes again."

Since then Cuddles has led Shaw down country roads, along moving sidewalks, and into airports and subways. "Let her choose the path," Janet Burleson told Shaw. "She always finds the safest route." On shopping trips, they even ride the escalators and elevators. "When I go to the mall and tell her to find the elevator, she will find it and push the button," says Shaw.

Cuddles has been taught 23 different voice commands. She can "wait" and go "forward." And she has been taught something called **intelligent disobedience**. Intelligent disobedience means that Cuddles will ignore a command from Shaw if it will put them in danger.

Dan Shaw's success with Cuddles has proven that a miniature horse can be a good guide animal. In fact, by October 2001 the Burlesons had a waiting list of more than 80 people who wanted a miniature guide horse. A miniature horse costs about $25,000 before it's even trained! The horses can be as young as 6 months old when they start training.

Not all horses that start in training end up as a guide horse. Twinkie, who was the Burlesons' first miniature horse, was not quick enough. Another horse named Nevada grew too big to fit under tables.

Today nine miniature horses are being trained at the foundation. Volunteers do all the training, which can take up to a year. When the miniature horse is ready, it is teamed up with a visually impaired person. This new person is called a handler. The pair train together at the foundation. Final training takes place at the handler's home. Cuddles and Dan Shaw are an example of a successful team. "She's everything I thought she'd be," Shaw says about his new guide horse. "When I first met her, we hit it right off. It was almost as if it was meant to be."

Cuddles and Dan go everywhere together.

Tian Tian and Mei Xiang
Hope for the Future

They're special visitors from China. They live at the National Zoo in Washington, D.C. They're black and white and furry. They're so popular that hundreds of fans visit them every day. Can you guess what they are?

If you guess "giant pandas," you are right! Tian Tian (t-YEN t-YEN) and Mei Xiang (may ZHONG) arrived in the United States on December 6, 2000. They will live in the United States for ten years and then go back to China.

Black and white, round and fuzzy, the pandas are so cute that people flock to the National Zoo to see them.

The National Zoo's first pair of pandas, Hsing-Hsing and Ling-Ling, had more than 70 million visitors!

While Tian and Mei are in the United States, scientists will study them. The giant panda, China's national symbol, is almost **extinct**. Pandas once roamed most of China. Scientists guess that less than 1000 pandas now live in the wild in China. China and the United States are working together to save the giant panda.

There are many reasons why the panda is becoming extinct. One reason is that pandas mostly eat bamboo, and China's bamboo forests are being destroyed. Even in the special panda parks, people continue to clear land for farms.

Another reason is that pandas give birth only once every two years. They have only one cub at a time, and many of the cubs don't **survive**. Many pandas in zoos don't have babies. Scientists don't know why. By studying Tian and Mei, scientists hope to learn more about the giant pandas. They hope to discover things that will keep the panda from becoming extinct. Tian Tian and Mei Xiang don't realize they are so important. They're more interested in being pandas.

A special **habitat** at the National Zoo keeps the pair active and healthy. The habitat has ponds, trees, and places to roll in the sand. It even has air-conditioned caves and misting sprays to help the wooly pandas stay cool in the summer. Bamboo grows in the habitat, too. Tian and Mei each eat about 50 pounds (23 kilograms) of bamboo a day! They also eat apples, carrots, and special biscuits.

Tian and Mei spend part of their day together. They love to wrestle with each other. Tian tackles Mei. She squeals, then tackles him.

Pandas are good at climbing.

Tian weighs about 250 pounds (114 kilograms). Mei weighs only about 200 pounds (91 kilograms). Even though Tian is bigger, he sometimes lets Mei win the play fights. When Tian gets too rough, Mei barks like a dog and then escapes up a willow tree or into her den.

The pandas also enjoy **enrichments** the keepers place in their habitat. An enrichment can be a sack filled with hay and biscuits or a water jug filled with apples. The pandas throw one of these around and shake it, trying to get to the food. But enrichments are not toys. In the wild, giant pandas spend much of their time searching for food and shelter. Enrichments encourage Tian and Mei to act more like wild pandas.

Tian Tian and Mei Xiang are still young, but scientists hope that one day they will mate and have cubs. The zoo's first pandas, Hsing-Hsing and Ling-Ling, never had a live cub. That was disappointing to everyone. We may need more pandas in zoos to help prevent the wild panda from becoming extinct. If Tian Tian and Mei Xiang do have a cub, it will belong to China. When the cub is old enough, it will probably go back to China to be part of their special panda program.

Tian Tian and Mei Xiang eat bamboo every day.

Thousands of visitors come to see Tian Tian and Mei Xiang at the zoo. Everyone loves the cute, cuddly-looking pandas. Students learn about the bears at school. Interested people watch the pandas on computers by clicking on the "PandaCams." Hundreds of fans send e-mail "Panda-Grams" like these:

A warm and friendly welcome to the cutest couple in Washington!

Hi, funny bears, . . . don't eat too much.

Hey, guys! Welcome to the neighborhood. Please, no loud parties.

Tian Tian and Mei Xiang may not know how special they are, but scientists do. They will continue to study these two rare animals to find out how to save all pandas.

Alex
The Famous Talking Parrot

Most of us know that parrots can whistle, bark like a dog, and imitate people. We know that sometimes they say, "Polly want a cracker." But have you ever heard of a parrot that can count to six? How about one that asks for his favorite food?

Meet Alex, the famous talking parrot. Alex can name about 100 objects. He can **identify** 7 colors, 5 shapes, and many materials such as wood and plastic. And he does these things in the English language!

Other animals have been taught to **communicate** with people. For example, apes have been taught sign language. Dolphins can push special symbols on boards.

But birds, especially parrots, are the only animals that can speak like a human.

For more than 20 years, Alex has worked with Dr. Irene Pepperberg at the University of Arizona. Dr. Pepperberg is an animal **biologist.** She studies animal communication. She tries to find the answers to questions such as Do animals talk to each other? Can they talk to people? Can they use language to get what they want? Alex is helping Dr. Pepperberg answer some of these questions.

Dr. Pepperberg bought Alex, an African gray parrot, from a Chicago pet store in 1977. Alex was 13 months old.

Alex can identify the colors and shapes of boxes.

Since then Dr. Pepperberg or one of her students has worked, talked, and played with Alex for 8 hours almost every day.

Dr. Pepperberg taught Alex in a special way. While Alex sat nearby, she held up a toy. Then a student named the toy. Dr. Pepperberg then handed it to the student. Alex listened and watched. It took time, but he learned that if he said the name of the toy, he got to play with it, too.

In his first 26 months with Dr. Pepperberg, Alex learned 9 names for objects, 3 color words, and 2 phrases. He also learned the word *no* and used it when he didn't want to do something. Since that time, Alex has learned many other words. When he is tired, he says, "Wanna go away." When he wants a treat, he says, "bread" or "grape" or "I want walnut." When he is bad, he says, "I'm sorry."

Alex cannot be tricked easily. If he asks for a banana but is given a nut, he might become angry and throw the nut away. Dr. Pepperberg says that Alex has also made up a word. He calls an apple a "bannery." He already knew the words *banana* and *cherry*. When she tried to teach him the word *apple*, he kept calling it a

Alex with Dr. Pepperberg, Griffen, and Kyaaro

bannery. Dr. Pepperberg says that Alex's new word makes sense. An apple is red like a cherry and tastes a little bit like a banana!

Dr. Pepperberg is now trying to teach Alex numbers. She hopes Alex will learn that the symbol *3* stands for three things. She is also trying to teach him sounds for letters. Then Alex could sound out words!

Alex is also helping to teach language to two other African gray parrots, Griffen and Kyaaro. The two young parrots watch while Alex works with a student. The student holds out a yellow key and a green key.

"What toy?" she asks Alex.

"Key," he answers.

"How many?"

"Two," he replies.

"What's different?"

"Color," he replies. Then he adds, "Cork nut," which means that he wants an almond.

The student gives Alex the almond for his reward. Dr. Pepperberg feels that Griffen and Kyaaro learn faster by watching Alex. If Griffen makes a mistake, Alex sometimes screeches, "Bad boy!"

Is Alex just imitating people? Or is he really communicating? Dr. Pepperberg replies, "I believe he thinks." After all, when Alex asks for a banana, that's what he really wants. She believes that he is as smart as a five- or six-year-old child. Alex's abilities haven't convinced everyone that he really understands and speaks English. However, most scientists agree that Alex means what he says!

Sugar
The Amazing Traveling Cat

The fluffy, cream-colored cat jumped through the barn window. She landed on Mrs. Woods's shoulder. Startled, Mrs. Woods cried out, "Sugar!"

But how could this cat be Sugar? More than a year earlier, Mr. and Mrs. Woods had moved to Oklahoma. They'd left Sugar behind with a neighbor in California. That was almost 1500 miles (2413 kilometers) away!

Still, Mrs. Woods thought this cat looked like Sugar. She had the same cream-colored fur and copper-colored eyes. Mrs. Woods knew there was one way to find out. Sugar had a **deformed** hip. Mrs. Woods felt the cat's hip. It was deformed. "Sugar," she said. "It *is* you."

Sugar may have traveled through Arizona, New Mexico, and Texas.

Sugar hated to ride in cars. That was the only reason the Woodses had left the cat behind when they moved. They felt that Sugar would be too scared to ride in the car for such a long way. They knew their neighbor would give Sugar a good home. When Mrs. Woods called the neighbor in California, the neighbor reported that Sugar had vanished two weeks after the Woodses left.

Mrs. Woods was still puzzled. To get to Oklahoma, Sugar would have had to travel 1500 miles (2413 kilometers). She would have had to cross deserts and climb mountains. She had no map or compass. She had never been to Oklahoma. How did Sugar find the Woodses' new farm?

Scientists heard about Sugar's amazing journey. Dr. J. B. Rhine wrote an article about it. He called Sugar's long trip an example of "psi-trailing." In psi-trailing, an animal is guided "by a still **unrecognized** means of knowing." What that means is that scientists have no idea how Sugar found her family!

There are other examples of cats like Sugar finding their owners over a long distance. Do they use odor clues? Do they have a special sense to guide them? Do they listen to signals from the earth? No one may ever know. But the Woodses do know that somehow Sugar found her way to their new home. It was surely an amazing journey.

Sugar traveled for months and months.

Kanzi
One Clever Ape

Covered with blankets, Kanzi hides from his caretaker. Worried, his caretaker hunts for him. Where is Kanzi? After 20 minutes, Kanzi throws back the blankets. He hoots happily, delighted at his caretaker's surprise. Kanzi loves to have fun. He watches himself in the mirror as he blows bubbles. When he wants to play a game, he tells his caretaker, "Keep away balloon."

Kanzi is a **bonobo,** a type of ape. Because he can't speak, he communicates using a special computer keyboard.

Bonobos are only found in the Congo, a country in Africa. They are similar to chimpanzees but smaller.

In the wild, bonobos live in the jungle. They live in peaceful groups. They call to each other in their own language. They even hug and kiss! Like the giant panda, they are an **endangered** species.

For years Kanzi has lived at Georgia State University in Atlanta. There Susan Savage-Rumbaugh and other scientists work with Kanzi and other bonobos. They are studying the bonobos to find out if they can understand and use words.

Apes can't speak like parrots, so they use a keyboard connected to a computer to communicate. The keyboard has symbols on it called **lexigrams.** A lexigram is a pattern or shape that means a word. When the ape hits a key, a lexigram lights up.

Headphones help Kanzi listen to words.

No one tried to teach Kanzi. He learned how to use the keyboard by watching his mother, Matata. When he was 18 months old, Kanzi began hitting the right keys to ask for things. By the time he was 4 years old, he was using 80 lexigrams. He pressed them to tell his teachers what he wanted. For example, Kanzi asked to go to the treehouse. His teacher told him, "Yes, we can go to the treehouse." Kanzi then led the teacher to the treehouse. In this way, Savage-Rumbaugh knew that Kanzi was using the keyboard to communicate.

Even more amazing, Kanzi understands spoken words and simple sentences. When he is asked to, Kanzi can put a ball in a bowl. He will carry the bowl to the refrigerator. Kanzi even signals to his teacher, "Kanzi be bad now," before taking another bonobo's banana. He understands language so well that his teachers spell out words they don't want him to hear! Dr. Savage-Rumbaugh feels that Kanzi understands language as well as a 2-year-old child.

One day Savage-Rumbaugh told Kanzi that there was a surprise for him. Kanzi thought it was food. But Savage-Rumbaugh told him, "No food surprise. Matata surprise." Matata and Kanzi had been separated for a while. Savage-Rumbaugh says that when Kanzi heard about his "Matata surprise," he looked stunned. Then Kanzi gestured for her to open the door so that he could see his mother.

Does Kanzi truly know language? Using the keyboard, Kanzi can ask and answer questions and invent games. He has shown again and again that he can use and understand words.

Kanzi lives at the Language Research Center in Atlanta, Georgia.

Snowman
A Cinderella Story

The horse at the Pennsylvania horse **auction** was dirty and rough-looking. Sold for $60, he was walking up a ramp into a van. The van was bound for a place that turned horses into food for dogs and into other products. But Harry de Leyer saw a spark of spirit in the gray horse's eye. Harry was looking for horses to use at the Knox School, where he taught riding. He wondered if he should take a chance on the dirty gray horse.

Harry asked the dealer to unload the horse. The gray horse was skinny. He had cuts and sores, too, but Harry liked him. The dealer accepted Harry's offer of $80, and the gray horse was given a second chance at life.

When Harry took the horse to his farm, one of his children said, "He looks just like a snowman!" The name stuck. The year was 1956. At that time no one knew that the horse bought for $80 would become one of the most famous show horses ever known.

Snowman started out as a lesson horse. He was so calm and sweet that all the students wanted to ride him. Harry's eight children also loved to ride Snowman. They swam the gray horse in the nearby bay and dove off his back into the water. When the school year was over, Harry sold Snowman to a doctor who wanted a quiet horse. Harry took the horse to the doctor's farm, which was two miles down the road.

One morning, Harry found Snowman back in his barn! He took the horse back to the doctor's farm. But every other night, Snowman jumped out of the doctor's **paddock.** "I would hear him clip-clop down the road," said Harry.

The doctor raised the fence in Snowman's paddock. Still the horse jumped out. Then the doctor tied a tire to a rope and attached the rope to Snowman's halter.

Snowman jumped the fence, pulled the tire over the fence boards, and dragged it all the way to the de Leyers' farm. Harry decided to buy Snowman back. After that the two were never parted.

Recognizing Snowman's jumping talent, Harry trained him as a jumper. "He was the smartest horse I ever taught," Harry later said. Snowman was a careful and willing jumper. In a horse show, a small child could ride him in a class. Then in the same show, Harry could jump him over 5-foot (1.5-meter) fences and win a blue ribbon for first place.

Soon Snowman was competing against the best horses in the best shows in the country—and winning! In 1958 and 1959, he was the American Horse Show Association Horse of the Year. During those same years, he won the Professional Horsemen's Association championship. In 1958 a horse magazine reported that Snowman had won almost $8,000 in prize money. That's like $50,000 today!

For five years, Snowman continued to win at shows. But Snowman also became "the people's horse." Snowman's rags-to-riches story touched everybody's heart. Children cried if he didn't win. He had his own fan club. People stood in line for hours just to meet him. School children took field trips to Harry's farm to see him. Snowman appeared on television and was the subject of two books. He even flew to Europe for guest appearances.

Snowman could even jump over another horse!

"The public understood his story," Harry said. "He was the underdog"—the one who was expected to lose at all of the shows. Instead he was beating all the famous horses at the biggest shows!

Snowman retired from show jumping but continued to tour and perform for audiences. In 1977 he died at the age of 28 at Harry's farm.

Snowman was made a member of the Show Jumping Hall of Fame in 1992. "Snowman was probably the most famous show horse ever known," said Harry. He was the Cinderella horse that everyone loved.

People loved to watch Snowman jump.

Ginny
A Cat's Best Friend

As Philip Gonzalez and Ginny walked past a city building, Ginny began to whimper. Philip knew what his dog's whimper meant. There was a cat or kitten to rescue!

Philip checked out the building, which was under construction. He couldn't see or hear anything that sounded like a cat. Ginny tugged at the leash. She knew there was a cat or kitten that needed saving.

Philip saw a guard. "There's nothing in there," the guard said. But Ginny stared at him with her big, pleading eyes, and the guard gave in. He unlocked the gate and let them into the building.

As soon as they were inside, Philip let go of Ginny's leash. She raced off. Minutes later, she came back holding a tiny kitten gently in her mouth. Philip took the kitten. It had a big scab on its face. It couldn't close its mouth. It was so weak it couldn't stand up.

Ginny was right. There *was* something in the building! Quickly Philip followed Ginny to the second floor. She went right to an air-conditioning duct. There Philip found several cats with kittens. When the mother cats saw Philip, they ran away. Philip checked out the other kittens. They were healthy. Ginny had found the only kitten that needed help.

Philip rushed the kitten to the **veterinarian.** "She's very sick," the vet said. He also said that she had a rare illness. She might not survive. If she did, she might not be able to walk. The vet said that Philip should put the kitten to sleep. But Philip and Ginny, who stayed by the kitten's side, wouldn't allow it. Philip told the vet not to put the kitten to sleep. She survived, and he named her Topsy. He calls her his miracle cat.

Topsy went home with Philip and Ginny. At the time, Philip lived in a small apartment with four other cats that Ginny rescued. There was Madame, a white

Ginny has rescued many cats.

cat who could not hear. Vogue was a stray who'd been **mistreated.** Revlon only had one eye. Betty Boop had no back feet. Ginny had found all of them.

Even though Topsy survived, she can't walk or stand up. She has learned how to roll wherever she wants to go. She even rolls in and out of her own house and litter box! After Topsy came home, Ginny found five other kittens. Someone had dropped them down a long pipe. They were only a week old and were covered with fleas and ticks. Philip and Ginny took them home.

Philip fed them special kitten food. Ginny groomed them to get rid of the fleas and ticks. They all survived!

Philip found good homes for two of the kittens. The other three stayed with Topsy, Vogue, Madame, Betty Boop, and Revlon. Now Ginny and Philip have eight cats. But Ginny is still finding more!

How does Ginny find cats that need rescuing? Philip says he believes that "Ginny can sense—in ways humans and other dogs cannot—pain, misery, fear, illness, injury, or **disability** in helpless cats, and move directly toward it to help." Philip Gonzalez calls this gift "radar of the heart." He should know. Ginny "rescued" him. Philip had hurt his arm in a terrible construction accident. Out of work, in pain, and feeling useless, Philip grew angry and lonely. Then a friend suggested he adopt a dog from the animal shelter. His trip to the shelter changed his mind and his life.

Ginny and her three puppies had been **abandoned.** At the shelter, she was waiting for someone to adopt her. Ginny was a funny-looking mutt with crooked legs, and at first, Philip didn't like her. He wanted a big dog that could protect him. But when they took a walk together, Ginny stopped on the sidewalk and looked up at Philip with her big bright eyes.

"I can't explain it," Philip says. "I only know that I was hooked instantly on that sweet little face." Then he added, "I had the strange feeling that we had known each other before, in a different time and place."

Philip chose Ginny to take home. Or had Ginny chosen Philip? Philip only knew that there was something special about Ginny.

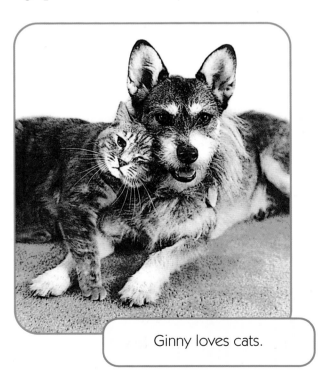

Ginny loves cats.

Ginny has thick fur because she is part husky.

Soon Philip discovered just how special Ginny was. Philip lived in the city, and he took Ginny for a walk early each morning. At the sight of a stray cat, Ginny tugged on her leash. She whimpered and danced, trying to get to it. One day, Ginny got loose. She ran up to a stray cat. She licked it, groomed it, and played with it. Philip was amazed!

Philip began feeding the stray cats that Ginny found. Soon he and Ginny became a team. Philip took any injured or sick cats to the vet. Then he tried to find them homes. Sometimes Ginny led Philip to a cat or kitten that really needed help. She found cats in trash cans and boxes of glass. Then Ginny whimpered to Philip until he helped the hurt cat.

Today Philip and Ginny continue to feed and rescue cats in their town. They have help from veterinarians and friends, but it is a huge job. For their good work, Ginny and Philip have received many awards. Ginny was even named Cat of the Year.

"I really do think Ginny is an angel," Philip says about his dog and her rescue work. "Where is it written that an angel must have wings and not a wagging tail?"

Glossary

abandoned (uh BAN duhnd) deserted; given up entirely

allergic (uh LUR jik) having an unusual reaction to things such as hair, food, or pollen

auction (AWK shin) a public sale at which something is sold to the person who offers the highest price for it

biologist (by AH luh jist) a scientist who studies living things

bonobo (buh NOH boh) a kind of small ape

communicate (kuh MYOO nuh kayt) to give or exchange information through talk, gestures, or writing

deformed (duh FAWRMD) misshapen

disability (DIS uh bil uh tee) something that weakens or cripples

endangered (en DAYN juhrd) to expose to harm or loss

enrichments (en RICH muhnts) things that make life better

extinct (ek STINKT) no longer existing; no longer on the earth

habitat (HAB uh tat) the place where an animal or plant naturally lives or grows

identify (iy DEN tuh fy) to recognize as being a particular person or thing

intelligent disobedience (in TEL uh juhnt dis uh BEE dee uhns) the deliberate ignoring of a command if it creates a risk

lexigrams (LEKS uh grams) patterns or shapes that stand for words

miniature (MIN uh chur) tiny

mistreated (mis TREET id) treated badly

obstacles (AHB stuh kuhlz) things that are in the way

paddock (PAD uhk) a small fenced-in field by a house or barn

survive (sur VYV) to continue to live and exist

unrecognized (uhn REK uhg nyzd) not identified or known

veterinarian (vet uhr uh NAIR ee uhn) a doctor who treats animals

visually impaired (VIZH yoo uhl ee im PAIRD) not able to see well

Index